How Lil' Eddie Learns to Read

Written by

Rima H. Corral

Synergy Books

How Lil' Eddie Learns to Read
Written by Rima H. Corral
Illustrations by Gerardo Barraza

Library of Congress Control Number: 2009933519

ISBN-13: 978-0-9840760-6-2
ISBN-10: 0-9840760-6-9

Published by Synergy Books
PO Box 80107
Austin, TX 78758

For more information about our books, please write to us, call 512.478.2028, or visit our website at www.synergybooks.net.

Production location: Nansha, Panyu, (Guangdong), China
Date of Production: 08/25/09
Cohort: Batch 1

10 9 8 7 6 5 4 3 2 1

This book is dedicated to my mother, Dora, who was determined that I would learn to read and write. She made sure I had everything I needed for school, which was not always easy. My ability to read and write and continue my education was of utmost importance to her because my mother could not read or write. With this ability, she believed I could grow up to be anything I wanted to be. These precious memories of my mother inspired me to write the words and music for my song, "You Can Be Anything You Want to Be." I love you, Mama. Thank you.

Thanks to my loving and supportive husband, retired Fire Chief Eddie Corral, and my sons, Eddie and Robert.

To my brother Ray Martinez, and my friends Joyce Jett, Walberto Martinez, Loreta Rea, and Dr. Ron Rea, whose support has been vital to me and so very much appreciated.

Dear Parents,

It is my greatest desire that this book will be fun and useful for you and your family. Consistency is the key here. It is best if mom, dad, brothers, and sisters can be involved in reading to your preschool child. Reading to your child has benefits beyond just learning to read. It builds a strong bond between you and your child as you share time together and you exclusively devote yourself to your child.

My experience as an educator of young children tells me they are eager to please their parents, even though they may sometimes appear reluctant. Reading is an activity that builds upon this affection and prepares children to acquire knowledge for life.

Research has shown that a child's reading readiness can be influenced by the advice given in the "Help for Parents" sections presented in this book and is not dependent solely on age. If your child is not ready to learn to read, a planned program of pre-reading activities is advised. The following will help: arts, crafts, music, dance, imaginative play, games, and visits and walks to libraries and museums. These types of experiences will stimulate your child to learn sooner. Explain to your child that if people cannot travel to other countries, they can always read about and experience an adventure as if they were in another country, through books.

I sincerely hope you enjoy the book and find "Help for Parents" useful and practical for you and your family. The concepts in "Help for Parents" will help to make your work a little easier. Your child should learn to read before he or she starts kindergarten, but it takes patience, consistency, and repetition. All children learn differently, so this book should be used and considered as a supplement to your current learning program.

My very best to you, whether you are a mom, dad, grandparent, foster parent, brother, sister, teacher, or another important person in a child's life. For the children, I have these special words, "My love, you can do it!" Good luck.

Your friend,

Rima

 # How Lil' Eddie Learns to Read

It was Saturday morning, and Lil' Eddie woke up at eight o'clock.
He was so excited because his mom had told him today was
his birthday. He was going to be three years old, and all of his
friends were coming to his birthday party.

His friends began to arrive for the party. They all brought him presents. Oh, what fun! There were birthday hats, balloons, and games. Madison brought her dog Ruby, who ran to play with Caitlyn's dog Cindy.

3

Lil' Eddie and his friends played all kinds of games: horseshoes, darts, hopscotch, and jump rope. The dogs were having fun running all over the place.

Then everybody lined up to take turns hitting the piñata. A piñata is a colorful container that everyone tries to break open with a broom while blindfolded.

This piñata hung from a tree and was in the shape of a big football. It was filled with candy and small toys. Everyone tried to break open the piñata, but no one had broken it yet. Then Lil' Eddie's cousin Wally hit the piñata hard, but nothing came out. Finally, Hanna, who was twelve years old and played softball at her school, hit the piñata so hard that candy and toys came flying out all over the place.

Oh! WOW! It was raining candy and toys. The boys and girls ran to pick up the goodies. "YEAA!" they shouted. "This is great!"

After the piñata, everyone gathered around Lil' Eddie and sang "Happy Birthday." He blew all three candles out on his birthday cake. "Way to go, Lil' Eddie," they shouted and clapped. Everyone ate pizza, hot dogs, and cake. Yum-yum!

Then it was time to open his twelve presents, exactly one dozen. He was so excited! He yelled, "Oh boy, oh boy," as he unwrapped toys and books about spelling and counting. It was a fun birthday party. Everyone had a good time.

Later that evening when everything was cleaned up and put away, Lil' Eddie's dad read a story to him, his sister, Caitlyn, and his brother, Robert. Everyone sat close together. They enjoyed the story because it was about a spaceship. After the story, it was time to say goodnight.

A few days later, Lil' Eddie's friends Ray and David came to play.
"Come on Lil' Eddie, let's ride your bike," said Ray. Both Ray and David
were almost five years old, so they knew how to ride. All three got along
well, and each boy took turns helping Lil' Eddie ride his bike. He soon
learned to ride his bike with training wheels.

One day, when Lil' Eddie was playing with his toys, he found the book David had given him for his birthday. Right away he liked the book with numbers. It had big, colorful pictures. He took the book to his mom so she could read it to him.

HELP FOR PARENTS

- When you first read to your child, explain what books are. I like to describe them as stories in writing. Explain how to use a book: how to hold it, how to open it (right to left). Talk about the different parts of the book: top, bottom, title, front cover, back cover, title page, and last page. Tell your child a little about the author and the illustrator.

- Reading begins by seeing words and hearing their sounds simultaneously. Point to each word as you read in a left to right progression.

- Family members can take turns reading to your child. Show picture cards and word cards three to five minutes at a time, not less than twice a day. Consistency and repetition is the key. This is how a child will begin to learn discipline. Always praise your child. Make it a fun time and show him or her your love.

Mom was happy Lil' Eddie had picked out the book he wanted her to read. She told him, "Good thinking. I like this book, too." Mom read the book about the numbers one to ten. When she finished she held up one hand and told him, "Remember, five is the number of fingers we have on each hand."

Then touching each finger of her right hand she counted, "One, two, three, four, five." She then held up her left hand and counted each finger, "Six, seven, eight, nine, ten." When she finished, Lil' Eddie smiled and tried to repeat what his mom had said. Then she showed him the picture of each number in the book: one apple, two oranges, three cars, and so on.

HELP FOR PARENTS

- **The more children know about what is being read to them, the more they will comprehend and want to learn.**

- **Teach your children songs and nursery rhymes that are fun to sing and say, like "Old MacDonald Had a Farm," "The Alphabet Song," and "Little Miss Muffet."**

- **Encourage your spouse or partner and older brothers and sisters to read to your younger child. Let your child hold the book and turn the page. Take your time reading. Do not rush. Tell your child to think about and imagine the story as you read it. Then ask your child to tell you about something he or she has done that is similar to the events in the story.**

Every day, Mom read the same book to him over and over. Then one day Lil' Eddie said, "Look Mommy, I have five fingers. One, two, three, four, five."

Mom was very excited. "You did it! You remembered exactly. Oh, I am so proud of you," she said as she hugged and kissed him.

17

HELP FOR PARENTS

- **Find a place in your home for a bookcase (within your child's reach), where books can be kept and stored after reading. Ask your child to find a book that he or she wants you to read and afterward have your child put the book back in its place on the shelf. This will teach your child about discipline, organization, and where things belong.**

- **If possible, let your child see you read every day. While working at home, read aloud grocery lists, invitations, phone numbers, and calendar dates.**

- **Help your child become aware that printed language is all around him or her on signs, billboards, and food labels, and in books, magazines, and newspapers. Point out the letters and words that you see everywhere; read aloud and spell the words found on traffic signs, street signs, store signs, etc.**

- **Talking about books on a regular basis shows children the benefits and pleasures of reading.**

The next day, Lil' Eddie's mom, being the creative, genius person she was, decided she would help Lil' Eddie learn to read. Hmmm, she thought. I will start very simply.

She talked to her family—Dad, Caitlyn, and Robert—about her plan and how they could help. Everyone agreed and was excited to help Lil' Eddie learn to read before he started kindergarten.

HELP FOR PARENTS

- **Start a neighborhood reading club where children get together regularly to share books and exchange stories. Have the children talk about the different things they can see, such as green leaves, or imagine hearing or feeling, such as falling rain and fuzzy caterpillars.**

- **Provide the children an opportunity to retell the story and playact the characters in the story. The repetition of different sounds and songs, as well as interaction with other children, are very important for developing your child's oral language, and ability to recall and understand events in a story. It also helps your child gain social skills.**

- **Read stories and poems aloud and have your child tell you about what he or she heard. Point out if a story has words that have the same sound (rhyming sounds). Examples: talking, walking, bat, cat. Depending on what the story is about, point out what is going on. Help your child recognize sounds that are loud, soft, pleasant, and scary.**

Part of Mom's plan was to have a reading group for the neighborhood children on Saturday mornings. On the first Saturday, Robert read a story about talking animals with very clear words and sounds. The children loved him because he was so funny. After Robert finished reading, Lil' Eddie's friends Lionel and Justin retold the story, and everyone acted out the characters. Everyone enjoyed the story time and looked forward to next week.

HELP FOR PARENTS

- The following activity will help with the memorization and recognition of letters. It will also supplement your child's effort in trying to match words to objects.

- Make flash cards of things your child likes to eat. No more than one thing per card: one apple, one banana, etc. Write the name of each food item underneath each picture, making no more than ten cards. Show the cards to your child; point to the picture, then the word, and spell it out. This activity must be repeated over and over.

- After practicing with cards containing both pictures and words, write only the words on another set of cards. Have your child match the picture/word card to the word-only card to learn and recognize words.

- At some point, your child may be able to match the picture with the word on his or her own. You must praise and praise your child! At this point, your child is trying to please you, and this positive reinforcement is how children gain the confidence to succeed in whatever they choose to do.

As Lil' Eddie grew a little older, he spoke more clearly and talked all the time. For his breakfast, Mom poured milk in a glass. She read and spelled the word "milk." Lil' Eddie repeated the word, "M-I-L-K."

She did the same with a box of cereal, pointing to the word on the box and spelling it. Lil' Eddie repeated the word, "C-E-R-E-A-L." Mom did this for the rest of breakfast and spelled the words bread, eggs, toast, juice, and bacon.

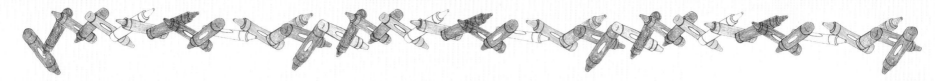

HELP FOR PARENTS

- Children demonstrate understanding through questions, comments, and actions. A child can do this by asking, Where? Why? How? When? What? Just be patient. Try to answer their questions with short answers. Eventually, your child will gain some understanding.

- Take your child to interesting places such as the zoo, a library, a park, a museum, or a shopping center. Point out what makes each place unique. Ask your child to tell you what he or she has learned and talk about the interesting places you have visited.

- Provide simple reading books and coloring books that show pictures of the places you visit, or make simple drawings your child can color.

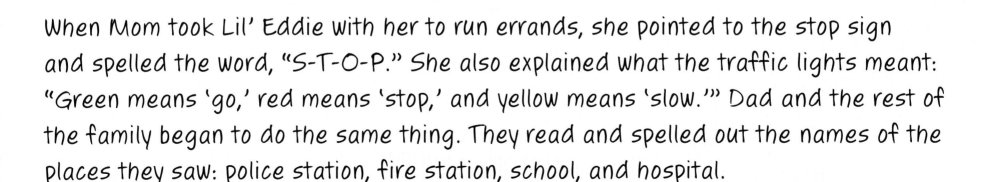

When Mom took Lil' Eddie with her to run errands, she pointed to the stop sign and spelled the word, "S-T-O-P." She also explained what the traffic lights meant: "Green means 'go,' red means 'stop,' and yellow means 'slow.'" Dad and the rest of the family began to do the same thing. They read and spelled out the names of the places they saw: police station, fire station, school, and hospital.

Lil' Eddie liked this. It was fun for him. He started spelling the words too. He decided right away that he wanted to be a firefighter. Mom took this opportunity to explain the significance and importance of 9-1-1 to Lil' Eddie, in case of an emergency.

HELP FOR PARENTS

- **Take your child to an art, science, or children's museum and point out different colors in paintings. Also, make him or her aware of the colors found in nature: green leaves, red flowers, and a blue sky.**

- **Point out different colored foods and their taste. Ask your child which taste and color he or she likes best. Everything is different, and that's okay!**

- **Give your child an opportunity to color different things. Remember that learning to stay inside the line when coloring will help your child learn to write and practice holding a pencil.**

Every day, Mom used the picture cards because Lil' Eddie liked to please her and the pictures made him laugh and talk more. Mom had picture cards with different colored foods that Lil' Eddie liked to eat, like a red apple, a yellow banana, and a piece of green celery. Mom also had pictures of other objects, like a brown snail, a blue truck, and an orange basketball.

Orange

Blue

Pink

Brown

Red

Purple

White

Yellow

Green

Lil' Eddie liked to color in his coloring book. He matched the objects in the pictures to their colors, and Mom taught him how to stay inside the lines when coloring.

HELP FOR PARENTS

- **Name an object. Help your child describe the object using adjectives and write down all of the words he or she comes up with, like smooth, rough, soft, or hard. Create simple sentences using the words.**

- **Practice identifying shapes by cutting out shapes that are round, square, triangular, and rectangular. Explain the different shapes to your child and where they appear.**

- **Have your child play with the shapes and make up pictures using a variety of them: a truck with wheels made from a rectangle and circles, a star made with triangles, etc.**

- **Help your child identify sounds made by certain animals, and then show him or her a picture of the animal. Let it be a colorful picture with the name of the animal—dog, cat, horse, etc.—written on it, so your child can begin to recognize how the word is spelled.**

Mom was careful not to make Lil' Eddie work too hard, although he liked matching the words and pictures over and over. She made flash cards with the words and pictures of things, like cereals, toys, pets, family members, stores, numbers, and shapes.

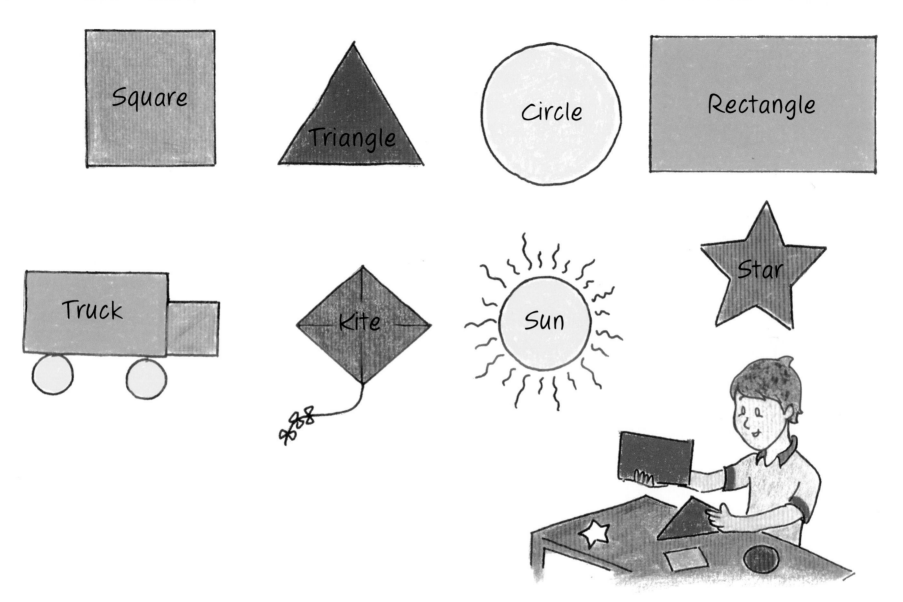

Square

Triangle

Circle

Rectangle

Truck

Kite

Sun

Star

Lil' Eddie really enjoyed this activity. He liked to play with the flash cards. He especially liked putting the different shapes together to form things such as cars, trucks, houses, and stars.

HELP FOR PARENTS

- **Provide crayons, paper, and capital and lowercase alphabet letters.**

- **Explain to your child that when writing his or her name, he or she should make the first letter a capital (big) letter, and then follow with lowercase (small) letters. Show him or her left to right progression.**

- **A person's name is usually written with a big first letter, then small letters. For example, "E-d-d-i-e." If a pre-kindergarten child is able to learn this way of writing his name, he will be ahead of the learning curve in kindergarten.**

- **Note: Some names, such as JoAnne, LaJoy, and DeeAnn, are exceptions to the rule.**

Lil' Eddie was now four and a half years old. He recognized the alphabet, big letters, and small letters. He sang the "Alphabet Song" all the time. One day he wanted to write his name. So Mom explained, "We always read and write from left to right.

Aa Bb Cc Dd Ee Ff Gg
Hh Ii Jj Kk Ll Mm Nn
Oo Pp Qq Rr Ss Tt Uu
Vv Ww Xx Yy Zz

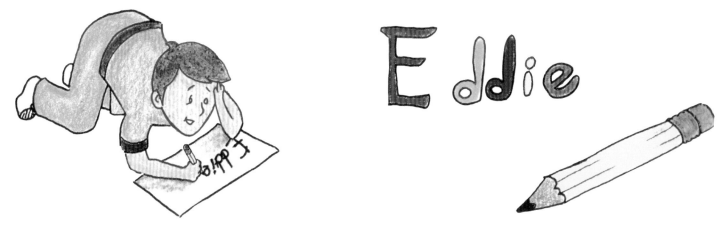

Eddie

The first letter of someone's name is written with a big letter, and the other letters are small." This is the way Lil' Eddie learned to write his name from the start.
E-d-d-i-e.

HELP FOR PARENTS

- Write "sight words" on flash cards. These are words a child will need to recognize by sight at some point, and some of these words will be found in every sentence: and, the, my, I, am, is, a, and to.

- Help your child identify sight words whenever possible. Say the word so he or she can hear the sound of each word.

- Make "sentence strips" by writing simple sentences on paper. No more than four to five words per sentence.

  Example: "My name is Eddie."

- Provide colorful books with four- to five-word sentences only.

Lil' Eddie tried to read. He picked up books and made up stories. One day Mom wrote some words on flash cards: the, my, I, am, is, a, and, to. "Some of these words are in just about every sentence you read," Mom told him. After a short time, Lil' Eddie learned these "sight words" and could read four- to five-word sentences.

So Mom wrote these short sentences, and Lil' Eddie could read them.

Example: My name is Eddie.

I am a boy.

The apple is red.

I go to school.

I like candy and cereal.

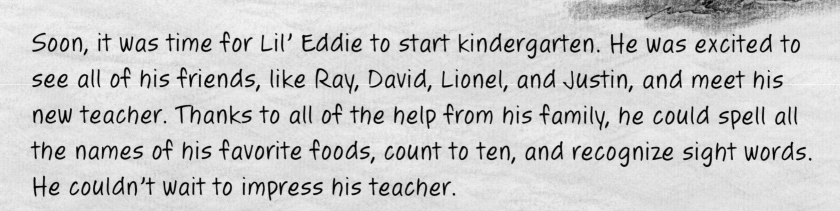

> Now I can read! Thank you Mom and Dad, sister Caitlyn, brother Robert, and my friends who helped me. Today is my first day at kindergarten and I am ready.

Soon, it was time for Lil' Eddie to start kindergarten. He was excited to see all of his friends, like Ray, David, Lionel, and Justin, and meet his new teacher. Thanks to all of the help from his family, he could spell all the names of his favorite foods, count to ten, and recognize sight words. He couldn't wait to impress his teacher.

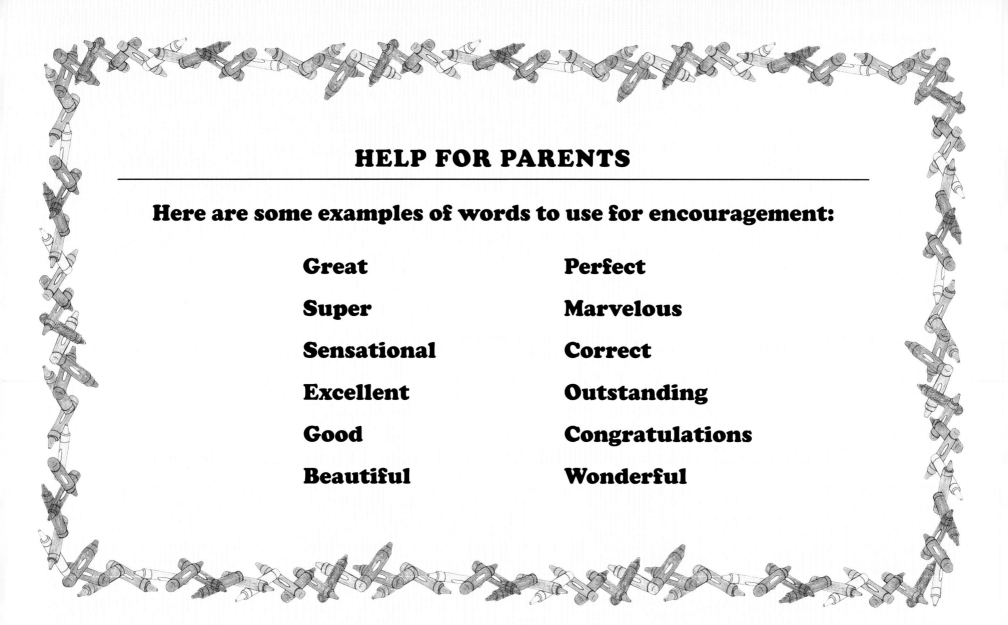

HELP FOR PARENTS

Here are some examples of words to use for encouragement:

Great	Perfect
Super	Marvelous
Sensational	Correct
Excellent	Outstanding
Good	Congratulations
Beautiful	Wonderful

HELP FOR PARENTS

Here are some examples of phrases to use for encouragement:

Now you have it!	**You did it that time!**
That's the way!	**Right on!**
You're doing fine.	**You really worked hard.**
You remembered!	**That's better than ever!**
I'm proud of you.	**I knew you could do it!**
Good for you!	**Keep up the good work.**

HELP FOR PARENTS

Suggested supplies to have on hand:

Markers

Crayons

Chalk

Pencils

Paper

Coloring books

Chalkboard

Flash cards

Picture books with one to two words per page

Picture books with four- and five-word sentences

Letters and numbers for tracing

Educator, singer, performer, author

ABOUT THE AUTHOR

Rima H. Corral is currently producer and creator of the children's television program, *Rima, Fuego and the Children*, which began as a local program on Houston PBS and now airs nationally. Rima is an Early Childhood Educator with twenty-five years of experience. She has a degree in Music and General Education, and several certifications. She is fluent in English and Spanish. This is her first book for children. She lives in Houston, Texas, with her husband and family.